"It really isn't fair, you know."

"Darlene isn't the best on the beam," complained Ashley. "It's just because of Darlene's dad that she's getting to be the star. I think it should be the best person, not the most famous daughter."

I know that most people think I get special treatment because of my dad. But here at gymnastics had always been the one place where that wasn't true. Until now.

Look for these and other books in THE GYMNASTS series:

THE GYMNASTS

#4 THE WINNER

Elizabeth Levy

AN
APPLE
PAPERBACK

SCHOLASTIC INC.
New York Toronto London Auckland Sydney

ISBN 0-590-41565-4

Copyright © 1989 by Elizabeth Levy. All rights reserved. Published by Scholastic Inc. APPLE PAPERBACKS is a registered trademark of Scholastic Inc. THE GYMNASTS is a trademark of Scholastic Inc.

12 11 10 9 8 7 6 5 4 3 2 1   9/8 0 1 2 3 4/9

Printed in the U.S.A.   28

First Scholastic printing, January 1989

Nobody Complains
a Rainbow Is Too Big

Most people call me Darlene, but some call me Big Foot. Nancy Drew wears a smaller size shoe than I do. She's supposed to be seventeen, and I'm only thirteen. The fact that I'm tall and have big feet would not be a big deal, except that I'm a gymnast. Gymnasts are supposed to be cute and petite. No one would ever call me petite, and cute has never been my style.

I'm already almost too tall for gymnastics. When I swing on the bars, my feet practically scrape the ground, even when the bars are put on a high setting. Patrick, my coach, keeps telling me that there are lots of gymnasts taller than me, but I don't see many of them. At least not many who are thirteen years old. I know judges like cute little gymnasts. Maybe that's why I've never won anything. I've come in second in a few events, but I never get a first — even sometimes when I think I've deserved it.

"Darlene," said Patrick. "As soon as you finish I've got a treat for you." I wondered if Patrick was teasing me. He knows I hate push-ups.

"Twenty more push-ups?" I asked, half grunting.

Patrick is my gymnastics coach at the Evergreen Gymnastics Academy. Some coaches run gymnastics like military school. I never did well with ones like that. Patrick is cool. He wants us to have fun. I like that in a coach. He also likes us to win.

"My treat is for after class," said Patrick. "A friend of mine and his wife have opened a new sports equipment company. They promised me a discount if I would let him bring their line over. I'm not endorsing any of his stuff, but I told him he could bring his van around today. He says he's got a new gymnastics shoe for only fifteen dollars. They're the same shoes that are worn by the Russian and Chinese teams."

I love clothes and shoes, and I love to shop. I have a bumper sticker stuck up on my wall at home that says it all: *When the Going Gets Tough, the Tough Go Shopping.*

I look at it this way: You go into a shop, you look around, and if you see something you like

2

and buy it, you make the salesperson happy, and you make the owner of the store happy. When you shop you spread a little happiness around.

I like to spread happiness around.

I was thinking about shopping when Patrick clapped his hands. "Darlene?" he asked. "Is that a push-up?"

I was lying on the mat with my elbows bent by my shoulders. Patrick wanted us to do twenty perfect push-ups before we were finished for the day. That's conditioning! I can remember the days before gymnastics when I thought conditioning was something that you did to your hair.

I straightened my elbows. Push-ups have always been hard for me. I just don't have much natural upper body strength. Patrick says that biceps are made, not born.

I glanced to my side. Lauren Baca's body was stiff as an ironing board as she lifted herself on her hands and her toes. She could do push-ups better than most boys. Lauren's compact, and she's a natural firecracker.

Patrick grabbed my hips and held them up. "Darlene, a push-up is not supposed to sag in the middle. That's why it's called a push-up, not a sag-up."

Ashley giggled. Lauren gave her a dirty look. Lauren is about the most loyal friend I could have.

I *think* Ashley giggled just to be playful, not mean. Ashley is new to the Evergreen Academy, and she doesn't quite fit in. Ashley is just a baby. She's only in third grade. She wears pigtails.

Ashley is too little to do real push-ups. Patrick lets her keep her knees on the mat. She finished way ahead of the rest of us and popped up to her feet.

"A sag-up," repeated Ashley. "I got to remember that." Patrick had moved on to correct someone else.

I sank back down on the mat.

"Why don't you just button up?" Lauren said to Ashley.

"Yeah? Who's going to make me?" said Ashley.

Now that has to be one of the stupidest things in the world to say. Ashley was just asking for it.

"Me, that's who," said Lauren. Lauren turned to face her. I put my hand on Lauren's arm. I hate fighting.

"Hey, cool it," I whispered, twisting my head toward Patrick.

Ashley stuck her tongue out at Lauren.

"That little twerp's giggle gets on my nerves," said Lauren.

"She's not so bad," I whispered. "She's just a baby."

"Yeah, she's as likeable as a baby rattlesnake," said Cindi Jockett.

4

"Naw," said Jodi Sutton. "Baby rattlesnakes are kind of sweet, with their little bitty rattles."

"Maybe we should give Ashley a baby rattle to wear around her neck to warn us when she's around," said Lauren.

Cindi, Lauren, Jodi, and me — we all started at Patrick's gym together. Jodi probably has the most experience. She was born into a gymnastics family. Her mother is a coach at Patrick's gym, although she doesn't coach us. But Jodi is not a great gymnast — yet. She's brave, but she's just not that skilled.

Cindi is probably the best all-around gymnast. She's been doing it for years. Lauren's got a lot of natural talent. She quit for a while, but now she's back doing it almost every day.

Basically, though, the four of us are all at about the same level. Patrick calls us his "Pinecones," and we are tight. I am the oldest, and I thought I'd feel funny with the others because I am just a little bit older. But I don't. It's not easy for me to make friends. I'm always worried that kids are just being nice to me because of my dad. Here, the only thing that counts is gymnastics, and the Pinecones became my friends long before they knew about my dad.

Sometimes I worry about us Pinecones. We're becoming a little bit of a clique. I've moved around a lot because of my dad's job, and I know how it feels to be the outsider. When I was real little, like Ashley's age, I made a vow to myself never to be part of a clique. But being part of the Pinecones has taught me something. It's so much fun to finally belong to a group that it's real easy to forget your vows.

Patrick clapped his hands again, signaling that our session was over. I rolled over on my back and rubbed my shoulders. We had been working on the bars all afternoon, and I felt like I had been stretched out on a rack. That's all I needed — to grow another few inches.

Patrick waved to a man rolling in two large suitcases on tiny wheels.

"There's my friend, Hugh," said Patrick. "He'll set up shop over there by the couches in the parents' lounge. Anybody who's interested in his gymnastics shoes can go there now."

"Let's go," said Cindi. "I want to get there first." I was surprised. Cindi hates to shop. It's all we can do to get her into a leotard. She likes to workout in shorts and big T-shirts.

"You?" I asked. "You're anxious to buy something?"

"I want to get it over with," said Cindi.

I shook my head. Now, that's an attitude I could never understand.

I picked up a pair of shoes. They were made of soft off-white leather. The leather was so soft I wanted to put it to my cheek just to feel its smoothness. The slippers had elastic on the tops and tough rubber soles that looked as if they would stick like suction cups to the beams.

I had to have a pair.

Becky was ahead of me. She's my age, but she wears a size five. I take a size nine. It's embarrassing. My shoes look like Cleopatra's barges.

"I bet they don't have these in my size," I said.

"What size do you take?" asked the man.

"Nine," I said.

"Sorry," he said. "I don't think the Chinese knew that gymnasts came in a size nine. The largest we have is a size eight."

"Maybe you can have your dad give these people a couple of footballs," said Becky. "They could turn those into shoes for you."

I could feel myself get hot. When I blush, it doesn't just go to my cheeks. I feel as if my whole body is turning different shades, like a science experiment in school.

Everyone knows about my dad, and anyone who knows me at all knows that I hate to be teased about him. My dad is a football player for the Denver Broncos. His real name is nice. Eric Broderick III. Doesn't that sound distinguished? But no one except my mom and my grandma call Dad Eric. Even his best friends call him "Beef." The media call him "Big Beef." He's had the nickname since grade school. He claims that he's had it before they even invented Big Macs.

Dad says that when he was growing up, the character he most resembled was Bill Cosby's Fat Albert. I guess I'm lucky that I'm not fat, but I sure inherited the "big" part.

"Footballs for shoes?" gasped Ashley. "That's a good one." Ashley nearly fell off her chair laughing.

The man selling the gymnastics slippers looked confused.

"She's Big Beef's daughter," said Ashley.

I wanted to sink through the floor. I hate it when people find out who I am. Perfectly normal people start acting crazy when they find out I've got a famous father.

"That's wonderful," said the man. I really wasn't sure what was so wonderful about it.

"Thanks," I muttered.

"I like the idea of you wearing footballs for slippers," said Becky. "Then all the judges will know right away that you're Big Beef's daughter."

I wanted to drop-kick her across the room. Becky is a good gymnast, but that's the nicest thing you can say about her. She's not part of the Pinecones. She's better than us, but just in gymnastics. Becky thinks she's better than us, period.

Becky goes to the same school that I do, St.

Agnes. It's a private school, and I know it's got a reputation for being snooty. Becky looks like she belongs on a St. Agnes brochure. She's got blonde, straight hair, and she's terminally preppy.

I'm black, and I definitely do not look like a miniature yuppie. I don't look like a miniature anything. Maybe that's why I like rainbows. Nobody ever complains that a rainbow is too big. I like color. I don't want to blend in with the woodwork.

2

"Sorry" Is My Least Favorite Word

About a week later we were working on the beam, and Ashley fell off — for the third time in a row. Patrick was very patient with her. You couldn't say that for the rest of us Pinecones. We were all peeved because Patrick had her working out with us, at least temporarily. At the gymnastics school where Ashley had gone before, she had specialized in tumbling and the vault. The truth was that already she was probably a better gymnast than any of the Pinecones, but she wasn't very good on the beam.

"Just what we need," muttered Lauren. "A miniature Becky on the beam."

"Well, Patrick's got to do what's best for everybody," I said.

Lauren widened her eyes. "Darlene, sometimes you are just too reasonable," she said.

I watched Ashley on the beam. Even though she didn't know exactly what she was doing, she was fun to watch. Some gymnasts just have charisma. You *want* to watch them. Ashley was one of those. With her two pigtails flopping up and down as she hopped across the beam, I couldn't take my eyes off her.

Dad says that you can always tell people with charisma. He says, "Even wearing our football helmets and all that padding, some good players just fade into the AstroTurf, and then there are ones who jump out at the crowd."

Dad is one of those who jumps out. The crowds have always loved Dad. When he plays football, he's like a lightning rod for the camera.

Dad says that guys who get noticed aren't necessarily better than the guys who don't. "We couldn't win games without the other guys, but charisma is the luck of the draw. If you've got it, you can get away with a lot less talent."

Watching Ashley I could see what he meant. Ashley didn't have all the skills that I had on the beam, at least not yet. But she was picking them up fast. She was going to be very good on the beam very soon.

But even if she wasn't the best, she made you want to keep your eyes on her.

Ashley looked like she was about to fall off, but she wasn't afraid of anything. I had a feeling that might be the secret of charisma — someone who just goes for it all. My dad plays like that.

Ashley fell off again, this time landing hard on her butt, but she just laughed. Patrick helped her to her feet. He patted the edge of the beam. "Ashley, focus on the end of the beam," he said. "Your eyes are going all over the place."

Ashley nodded and hopped right back on the beam. I have to give her credit. Falling off doesn't seem to embarrass her.

Lauren bounced impatiently on her toes next to me. We were still waiting for our turn. Patrick *was* taking a very long time with Ashley. I didn't blame Lauren for getting restless. "I wish Patrick hadn't put her with our group," said Lauren, touching her toes to stretch out. I massaged Lauren's lower back to help her get closer to the floor.

"You've got to admit Ashley has talent," I said. "The judges are going to love her."

"Who are the judges going to love?" asked Cindi, coming up to us. I bent down and touched my toes, and Cindi pushed on my lower back. We Pinecones are always helping each other out like that.

"Ashley," said Lauren. "Ashley the Bounce. She's so bouncy. She makes me sick. She keeps smiling at Patrick as if she's on TV."

Ashley tried to do a forward roll on the beam but her hips were off-center and she fell off. Patrick tried to catch her, but she was already too far gone. She kind of slipped into a pile of giggles on the mat.

Patrick laughed. "Okay, giggle-puss," he said. "That's enough for a while. I'm getting exhausted just counting your falls."

"If she were doing a routine, she'd be in the negative numbers," muttered Lauren.

Patrick heard her. "Ashley doesn't have the experience on the beam that you kids have, but she's got all the tumbling moves. I have a feeling she's going to be incredible." Patrick patted Ashley on the back. She flashed a huge grin at him.

"Yeah, the incredible, inedible bounce," said Lauren. "She gives me indigestion."

"Darlene," said Patrick. "It's your turn."

I love the beam. It's my favorite event. I know some gymnasts hate it. Lauren, for example, thinks of the beam as a threat. She's always sure that in any meet she's going to fall off.

I fall off sometimes, but I know I look good on the beam. It's the one event where it doesn't matter that I'm tall. I've been taking ballet since I was about six, and all that dance training really helps on the beam. Patrick is always telling us to imagine that someone is pulling us up by the armpits. All those years of ballet have taught me to pull up.

I did a body wave. It's one of the required moves in my routine. I tried to uncurl my body like a wave. It's hard to do it gracefully. Doing a body wave on the beam is like trying to do one of the dance moves from *Dirty Dancing* on a tightrope.

I thought I did a good body wave. I did a leap. Patrick had one hand on his chin, studying me critically.

I did my tuck jump, tucking my feet underneath me and lifting my arms. Then I did my curtsy, twisting slightly to the right.

"Stop, Darlene," said Patrick.

"What's wrong?" I asked, balancing on the beam. I turned to face him.

"Nothing, you're doing each element fine. But it doesn't have flair. Your eyes are always on the end of the beam. You never look up."

"But that's what you taught us to do," I complained. "You always say look at the end of the beam. That's what you just said to Ashley."

"That's for Ashley. She's getting used to the beam. But you're more experienced. Give me a reason to look at you up there. Use your eyes to bring the judges and the audience close to you. If you're looking at us, we'll look at you. Think of your favorite rock star. I'm sure she's always looking out at the audience, picking one or two faces to sing to. That's how great performers act. You've got to think of the beam as theater on a stick."

Ashley giggled. I did, too.

"Theater on a stick?" I repeated. "What does that make me? A Popsicle?"

Patrick didn't laugh. "I read that in Bill Sands' book on coaching girls. It's a good image. You're an actress up there. You're in the spotlight. You've got to act like you belong."

"Personally I think it's hard enough just staying up on the beam," I said.

Patrick shook his head. "Nope. Not for you. In fact, now that I think about it, you don't fall off enough. Ashley falls off a lot because she's trying too hard. You're too cautious on the beam. I'd like it if you fell off more."

Patrick was making me mad. "*Moi!??* Too cautious?" I exclaimed.

"You," said Patrick. He patted the beam. "Hop off and start again."

I jumped off, nearly tripping on my big feet as I landed.

"Very graceful," said Patrick, helping me up.

"Sorry," I mumbled.

Patrick smiled at me. "That's one of my least favorite words," he said.

"Sorry," I said again. Then I put my hand over my mouth. "Whoops, sorry."

"Three sorries in a row," said Patrick. "I think I'm going to fine you for every time you say 'sorry.' "

I looked at him to see if he was kidding. He was grinning, but I felt a little crushed.

"Sorry" is one of my least favorite words, too. I say it too often. Sometimes I say it without thinking. If someone bumps into me, chances are, I'm the one who says "I'm sorry."

"Come on, Darlene, concentrate. Let's see you do a cartwheel. I'll spot you."

I got back on the beam. I'm just learning to do a cartwheel on the beam. It's hard because if you don't land exactly right, you fall off quickly. I definitely needed Patrick to spot me. I wasn't ready to try it by myself.

I started my lunge. Patrick put his hand up, indicating that I should do it, but he wasn't looking at me. He was staring at the front door. Suddenly the gym was quiet. I stood back up and looked around to see what everyone was staring at.

It was my father. He was standing in the doorway to the gym with Darryl Collins and Al Botkin, two of his teammates, behind him. No way could the three of them have ever gotten through the

16

door side by side. They'd have to tear it down.

Dad waved at me. That's when I fell off. Dad was supposed to be at football practice. What was he doing in *my* gym with a bunch of Denver Broncos?

3

Too Much Adventure?

I'm used to my dad. Now that may sound like an obvious statement, right? Everybody's used to their dad. But believe me, most dads do not look like my father. People stare at him even when they don't know that he's a football star. It's not just that he's so much bigger than everybody else; he's got a wide forehead and high cheekbones. My dad is so handsome he gets stares even sitting down.

So, as I say, I'm used to everything stopping when Dad enters a room.

But Dad alone is nothing compared to the effect when you put two or three professional football players together. It's like some kind of scientific explosion. One plus one doesn't equal two. Putting three football players in a room full of gymnasts makes everyone else look like Pee-wee Herman.

Even Patrick looked tiny. Patrick's so incredibly muscled that I forget he's short. But standing next to my dad, shaking hands with Darryl and Al, he looked like a little kid.

Jodi's mother stopped what she was doing and went over to my dad with a big grin on her face.

"Is that your dad?" Ashley asked. "He's awesome."

"I don't know what he's doing here," I mumbled.

"To see us," said Cindi. Cindi likes my dad, and not just because he's famous. "Let's go say hello."

We all went over to them. Dad put his arm around me. "Hi, honey."

I introduced the Pinecones to the other Broncos. "Have you guys decided to take up gymnastics?" Lauren asked.

"They'd break the beam," Ashley whispered.

Dad heard her and laughed. "You're probably right."

Lauren looked serious. "No, Ashley's wrong. The beam could hold you. It's a proven fact that the beam can take thousands of pounds of pressure because of all the jumps we do on it."

"A proven fact," repeated Dad.

"Hey, Beef," said Darryl. "Maybe we should get up on the beam."

"It might not be a bad idea," said Patrick. "Don't some football players take ballet?"

Darryl nodded. "Yeah, Herschel Walker even performed with the Dallas Ballet."

Dad slapped Patrick on his back. "How about it? You can call us the 'Redwoods' instead of the Pinecones."

"I like it," said Patrick. "Is that really why you guys came here?" Patrick took in my dad's six-feet-four frame and two hundred and forty pounds. "I think I'll have to change the fittings on the uneven bars for you."

I giggled. The idea of my dad swinging around on the bars made me laugh.

Dad winked at me. "I think beam would be more my style. Isn't that Darlene's best event?"

Patrick nodded.

"Well, that's what I came to talk to you about," said my dad.

I got nervous. I hoped Dad hadn't come to talk to Patrick about why I wasn't in a more advanced group. I'd die of embarrassment if he did that. Dad teases me about the fact that all the Pinecones are younger than me. But I'd fall through the floor if he brought that up in public.

Patrick coughed. He nodded toward Darryl and

Al. "What do you want to talk to me about?" Patrick asked. "You gotta admit it's a little intimidating when a parent comes to talk to me, and he brings two big guys to do it."

"No, no . . . I've come to ask you a favor," said Dad. "Darryl and Al came because they're involved, too."

Patrick looked confused. "What's the favor?" he asked.

Dad gave me a little hug. "I think you're going to like this, Darlene."

I got a little nervous when I heard that. Dad loves to spring surprises on me. Sometimes the surprises are a little hard to take.

"What exactly is it that I'm gonna like?" I asked warily.

"The Broncos want to do a halftime show saluting the young athletes of the city," Dad explained. "At first they were just going to go with the team sports — Little League teams, a group from the PeeWee football league. Darryl and Al both have sons who are going to be in the show. The Broncos decided they'd like to include as many of the sons and daughters of the players as they could. I told them they should include some individual sports. They agreed to feature one gymnast. I described how cute Darlene looks on the beam, and they like the idea of having my daughter featured. They'd also like the rest of the Pinecones to do a little tumbling, but they'll feature Darlene."

Dad looked down at me. "I came right over after I found out that they wanted to put you in the show."

"I think it's a terrific idea," said Patrick. "It'll be a blast. I'll help Darlene work up a great routine on the beam. We'll feature all the things she's best at."

"Wait a minute," I said. "Won't the rest of the Pinecones be jealous?"

"You've got to be kidding," said Cindi, jumping up and down. "Why should we be jealous? You heard your dad. We're gonna do a little tumbling, too. We'll get to be in a halftime show. Can my brothers come to the game?"

"Absolutely," said my dad. "I'll make sure that the families of all the girls get tickets."

"All right!" said Jodi. Even her mom looked pleased. Broncos tickets are harder to get than seats for a Springsteen concert.

"I'll get seats for all of you," said Dad. "And the announcer will make it clear that it's the Pinecones from Patrick Harmon's Evergreen Gymnastics Academy."

Jodi's mother was grinning from ear to ear. "Not bad publicity, eh, Patrick?"

I was surprised to see Patrick blushing. "Not bad at all," he admitted.

"Darlene, what do you say?" asked Patrick.

My heart was beating a mile a minute. Me in a halftime show, up on the beam, in the spotlight. It would be great. Terrifying, but great.

I saw Dad giving me a worried look. It's funny how every once in a while I know exactly what he's thinking. He was scared that maybe he *had* embarrassed me, that I'd be mad at him for not asking me first.

But Dad knew me too well. He knew that if he had asked me first, I might have stalled and said "Aw, shucks! Why don't they pick somebody else?"

Now it was a *fait accompli,* as they say. Dad just came out and blurted it out in front of everybody. Now I couldn't back down. And I was glad.

"Come on, Darlene," urged Lauren. "What do you say?"

"What does she say?" squealed Cindi. "She says okay. It's the most exciting idea in the twentieth century!"

"I wouldn't go *that* far," I said. "But it sounds neat, Dad."

"Neat?" shrieked Cindi. "You're going to perform in front of thousands and thousands of people and all you can say is 'neat'?"

I wished Cindi would just shut up about the thousands and thousands of people. What if I fell in front of thousands and thousands of people?

Dad hugged me. "Does it scare you a little?" he asked.

I nodded.

"Everyone will love you," said Dad. "They're not expecting a professional. There'll be lots of kids in the show."

"But Darlene will be the only one doing the beam?" asked Lauren.

"Won't she be too small for everyone to see?" asked Ashley. "Wouldn't it be better if we all did something?"

Dad looked down at us all. "Even all of you standing end to end wouldn't show up on the football field. They'll televise it live on the stadium screen."

I swallowed hard. The more I heard about this, the scarier it got.

Dad looked into my eyes. "You're not mad at me for not asking you privately?" he whispered.

I shook my head. I really wasn't. If Dad had asked me confidentially I might have said no. Sometimes I say no to things that I really want to do because I'm scared and then I'm sorry.

But this way it was already all set. I didn't even have to try out or anything.

Patrick shook hands with Darryl and Al.

24

"Do you want to watch for a while?" he asked. "I was just working on Darlene's cartwheel on the beam."

Dad glanced at Darryl and Al, who nodded.

"Come on," said Patrick. "Let's get back to work."

My heart was racing. If I was terrified of performing in front of my dad and two men I knew, how was I going to survive performing in front of thousands of people? I told myself to calm down.

Patrick gave me a reassuring grin.

I did a good tuck-vault mount onto the beam, and then I did one of my body waves.

I heard Darryl applaud. Now I was feeling a little more confident.

"Try the cartwheel," said Patrick.

I licked my lips.

"Okay," I muttered. I found my balance and did my preparatory lunge. Then I put my hands down and kicked my legs above me. Patrick caught my waist and helped me get my feet down on the beam.

"Of course, if we want to add that to the half-time show, you'll have to do it without a spot," said Patrick. "But you can do it. You're almost there now."

"I'll work on it," I promised.

"Do me a favor this weekend," said Patrick.

"Work on your beam routine. Tell me on Monday which parts you want to put in the show."

"Okay," I said.

" 'The show.' " Patrick said it too casually. I hopped off the beam and went over to my father.

"I'm scared to death I'll make a fool of myself," I said.

"Don't worry," said Dad. "You looked terrific."

"You were just great," said Darryl.

It was easy for them to say that. They didn't know how nervous I was just performing in front of them.

It was going to be hair-raising trying to get up my nerve to do it in the stadium. But this was going to be exciting. It would definitely be an adventure.

Is there such a thing as too much adventure?

4

Have You Ever Been a Winner?

"You're too nice to her," complained Cindi. "Why is she coming over?"

"How could I invite the Pinecones and not invite her?" I argued.

"She is not a Pinecone," said Cindi. "She is a twerp."

It was Saturday. All the Pinecones were coming over to my house to help me work out a routine on the beam, and I had invited Ashley.

"She was standing right there when I invited you," I said to Cindi. "I couldn't not invite her."

"Who's her?" asked Dad. "Becky the witch?"

"No, Ashley. She's a Becky-in-training," said Cindi. "She's only nine years old, and she's a little snot."

27

"You met her at the gym," I said.

"I don't remember her," said Dad. Now why did that secretly please me?

"She's definitely not worth remembering," Cindi said.

"I think we're all being unfair to her," I said.

"Sometimes you're too fair," said Cindi.

Dad glanced at Cindi. "Do you really think there's such a thing as being too fair?" he asked.

"Well, sometimes Darlene is just too nice," said Cindi.

"I don't think her little sisters would agree with you," said Dad.

Cindi had gotten to my house early. Her brother Tim drove her, and then he stayed to hang out. Tim always likes to be around when my dad's at home. The Broncos were playing at home tomorrow. The day before a game, Dad is always keyed up, but at the same time, he's supposed to relax. He always prowls around the house, looking for something to do. Usually he cooks. Today he had promised the Pinecones an old-fashioned barbecue. Dad says cooking soothes him. Mom says that he does it just to make a mess.

My little sister Deirdre toddled into the room holding on to my other little sister, Debi. Deirdre is only fourteen months old and Debi is four, and I've got to admit that the two of them looked adorable. Debi is really cute-looking. She's got a huge head of hair and big brown eyes and a button nose. She's got a crush on Cindi's brother Tim. Every time she sees him, she makes goo-goo eyes at him and gives him a big smile.

"How's my girlfriend?"asked Tim.

"I'm fine," said Debi in a precious voice. "So's Deirdre. She's just learning to walk."

Tim lifted Deirdre high in the air. "I can remember when Cindi was your size. We used to toss her around like a football."

"You still would if you got the chance," said Cindi.

Dad wiped his hands on his apron. "Let me have her," he said. "Lateral pass."

Dad's an offensive lineman and he doesn't catch passes, not unless there's been a major screw-up, but it has happened.

Deirdre looked tiny in his hands. She squealed happily.

"I want to be a football! I want to be a football!" squeaked Debi.

Tim picked her up.

Darlene, Debi, and Deirdre. My parents got stuck on the letter D. I'm named for my mom's grandmother, who died before I was born. I hate my name. In kindergarten I got the nickname,

"Mean Darlene," not 'cause I'm so mean but just because it rhymed.

The doorbell rang. It was Ashley. She *would* have to arrive early. I wondered where Lauren and Jodi were.

"Your house is so neat," exclaimed Ashley before she had even gotten through the front door.

I know our house is pretty spectacular and all that. Mom's got great taste. Everything in the house is big so that it fits Dad's size, but it doesn't feel like a house in a magazine. Mom loves sunlight, and every room has a slanting skylight that's electrified to melt the snow.

"Come on in," I said.

"My friends at school couldn't believe that I was going over to Big Beef's house," said Ashley.

"It's my house, too," I said.

Just then I saw a car pull into the driveway. Lauren and Jodi piled out. They pushed past Ashley.

"Hi ya, Darlene," shouted Jodi. "Looking good." Jodi walked into the house without making a fuss. It's true she had been there before, but none of the Pinecones had ever made me feel like part of a freak show just because my dad is famous.

Ashley seemed like a kid who only wanted to be my friend so she could talk about it later.

30

We all went into the kitchen. "Oh, no," said Dad. "A gaggle of gymnasts. Or is it a giggle of gymnasts?"

Ashley giggled loudly, a little too loudly, I thought.

"A gaggle is for geese," said Lauren.

"Well, there should be a name for what happens when gymnasts get together," said Dad.

"There is," said Cindi. "It's PINECONES."

"But that's only for you guys," said Ashley. "I'm not officially a Pinecone."

"Right," snickered Lauren. "You're not."

"If I'm not a Pinecone, then Pinecones can't be the name for a group of gymnasts, can it? 'Cause I'm a gymnast, too." Ashley whined. She sounded, well, she sounded like a nine-year-old, and not a very bright one at that.

"Let's go downstairs," I said, wanting to change the subject. I might not like Ashley, but she *was* a guest. I didn't want to be too cruel to her.

"Good idea," said my dad. "I have to perfect my sauce."

"I like it hot," said Jodi.

"Don't worry," I said. "Dad's barbecue sauce is sometimes so spicy we need to call the fire department."

"It's not just three-alarm . . . it's five-alarm," added Mom.

"That's how I like it," said Jodi.

"I've seen you perform at your meets, Jodi," said Dad. "I can tell you like taking chances."

"Sometimes too many," said Lauren.

"I like to take chances, too," piped up Ashley.

Everything that little pipsqueak was saying was getting on my nerves, but I guess it really wasn't her fault. I was getting as bad as the rest of the Pinecones.

We went downstairs to the gym. Dad has his own set of Nautilus equipment and free weights down there. I had gotten my parents to put in a beam for me, and some mats for tumbling.

"I don't believe this!" exclaimed Ashley. "This is terrific!"

She did a cartwheel on one of the mats. "Boy, if I had this equipment I'd be number one. How come you're not better?"

Cindi winked at me. "Just a simple, sweet question."

Ashley looked hurt. "What did I say? I just wondered if maybe Darlene hated to practice or something. She's got all this equipment and all the advantages. She's so lucky, it's incredible."

"Its rude to ask her how come she's not so much better," said Lauren angrily.

"I didn't mean to hurt your feelings," muttered Ashley. "It just seems so unfair."

"What seems unfair?" asked Lauren, still sounding angry.

"I mean, Darlene gets everything handed to her." Ashley looked up at me with her innocent blue eyes. "You live in this fantastic house. You have all this equipment to practice on. Your dad's a big football hero and he makes a fortune. You're gonna get to star in the halftime show, and you didn't have to win anything or try out for it."

"Darlene is great on the beam," said Jodi. "When we had a meet with the Atomic Amazons, *before* you showed up on the scene, Darlene got the highest score of any of us."

"Yeah, but the Atomic Amazons got all the medals," I admitted. "I didn't even place."

"Have you ever been a winner?" Ashley asked. Little Miss Cunning.

I stared at her. This little twerp was some piece of work. But she was asking all the right questions. Had I ever been a winner?

Luckily, before I had to answer her, Dad called us to come on up for lunch.

"Don't pay any attention to her," Lauren whispered to me. "She must have grown up in a box. She's the rudest thing on two legs."

"She's just a baby," I said.

"Yeah, a baby viper," said Jodi.

But I couldn't put Ashley's comment out of my mind. Was everyone thinking it was unfair that I had been picked just because I was my father's daughter?

The other Pinecones were so loyal and quick to come to my defense. But what about when I wasn't around? Did they secretly think it wasn't fair? After all, I knew the answer to Ashley's question. Had I ever been a winner? No.

5

Mean Darlene

"It really isn't fair, you know. Darlene isn't the best on the beam. You're much better." I heard Ashley's high-pitched voice and I wondered who she was talking to. It is definitely weird to eavesdrop on people talking about you.

It was the Monday following our barbecue, and I was in the bathroom in the locker room. Ashley and someone else were talking. I couldn't tell who else. I guess I could have burst out of the stall and announced myself. But there is something fascinating about hearing your name mentioned when people don't know you are listening. It sort of paralyzed me. I put my feet on top of the toilet seat so that it would look empty if anyone peeked under the door.

"I know I'm much better," said the other person. I recognized Becky's voice. Of course, she would say she was better. "But only the precious Pinecones are getting to be in the halftime show," continued Becky. "I'm surprised Darlene is even letting you go on the field with her."

"All we're going to do is a few cartwheels and handsprings. Then *she* gets to go on the beam."

I heard someone else come into the bathroom. "Darlene does look pretty good on the beam," Becky admitted. "It's her best event." I was surprised to hear her say anything nice about me.

"Yeah, but pretty good shouldn't be enough to get you singled out," complained Ashley. "It's because of Darlene's dad that she's getting to be the star. I think it should be the best person, not the most famous daughter."

"We wouldn't be going at all if it weren't for Darlene's dad." I recognized Cindi's voice. No wonder Becky had suddenly said something nice about me. It must have been just as Cindi walked in.

"Now that I think about it," said Becky, "I agree with Ashley. I think it's going to be kind of embarrassing having Darlene represent the Pinecones. After all, it'll be announced that you all train with Patrick. I mean, it'll be in front of fifty thousand people. You know Darlene gets 'performance anxiety' even in a small meet."

"Performance anxiety?" said Cindi. "Where did you get that?"

"Patrick talked to me about it." said Becky. "He used Darlene as an example of someone who's always good in practice, and then under pressure she crumbles. You know she'll fall off and then she'll get all flustered. It'll be excruciating."

"I just don't see why the spotlight should be on Darlene if she's not the best," whined Ashley. "It's mean. No wonder everyone calls her Mean Darlene."

Oh, no, I thought to myself — not *that* old nickname. Nobody had called me that to my face in years. I hate that nickname.

"Nobody calls her that," said Cindi angrily.

"I made it up," said Ashley. "I think it fits her." I wanted to throttle that little pipsqueak.

"But Darlene's never mean," argued Cindi.

"It rhymes," said Becky, drawling out the words.

I hugged my knees and bit my knuckle. This was awful. I wished then that I hadn't hidden. But it was too late to come out. I couldn't come out after hearing all that.

"After all, Cindi, even you are better than Darlene," said Becky.

"Even me?" asked Cindi. "You've got a great way with a compliment."

"Well, you know what she means," said Ashley.

"It's true, Cindi, you usually score higher than Darlene at meets," said Becky. "I don't think Darlene's ever won anything in her life. Tell the truth. Haven't you always scored higher than Darlene?"

"Not absolutely always," said Cindi. "Darlene did real well against the Atomic Amazons on the beam."

"Well, I still think that in a fair contest, either you or Ashley would score higher," said Becky. "Ashley's been improving a mile a minute on the beam."

"But this isn't a fair contest," said Cindi. "Come on. Let's go. Patrick's waiting for us."

I cringed. Even Cindi, a Pinecone, thought that it wasn't fair.

6

Just Never Mind! Never Mind!

I waited until I heard the door close before I lowered my legs. On of my calves had knotted up. I massaged it, remembering Cindi's words. "But this isn't a fair contest."

I couldn't believe Cindi had said that. I know that most people think I get special treatment because of my dad. But here at gymnastics had always been the one place where that wasn't true. Until now.

I was so stupid. I should never have agreed to star in the halftime show. I should have known that everybody would be jealous. Somehow when Dad first suggested it, it had seemed natural that it would be me. Dad had a way of making everything he wanted seem natural.

39

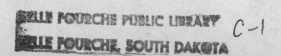

But now that I thought about it, it wasn't fair.

I walked out into the main part of the locker room. Cindi waved to me. I waved back, but it was a halfhearted wave.

"Look alive, Darlene," said Jodi. "Are you ready for the workout of a lifetime? I heard Mom talking to Patrick about what they wanted you to do for the Broncos' show. It's gonna be a doozy."

"Great," I mumbled. "I won't be able to do half of it."

"Well, *you're* in a good mood," said Jodi sarcastically.

"Yeah, Darlene," said Cindi. "You'd better snap out of your funk. Remember you're going to be representing *all* the Pinecones out there. We don't want you to foul up. We want you to practice, practice, practice until you're perfect."

"Maybe you'd rather have someone else up there," I said, putting on my leotard.

"Nobody else is a Bronco's daughter," said Cindi.

"That doesn't make it *fair*," I said, emphasizing the word fair. "Maybe I won't do it."

"What is she talking about?" Ashley asked.

Cindi looked angry. "That's ridiculous, Darlene. It's all settled. You're starring in the half-time show."

"Yeah," agreed Jodi. "You can't back out now."

I shook my head. "Patrick should pick Ashley or Cindi. They're the best."

"But Big Beef is your dad," argued Cindi. "I don't belong up there, and neither does Ashley."

"I agree," said Jodi.

Cindi turned to her. I had a feeling that Cindi hadn't expected Jodi to agree quite so quickly.

"Cindi, you and Ashley are tiny. You would be lost in the big stadium," explained Jodi.

"I would not get lost,"said Ashley.

"I said *be* lost, not *get* lost," said Jodi. "Although that's not a bad idea. You're so tiny that if they featured you, nobody would see you."

"They would too see me," said Ashley.

"You?" teased Jodi. "You'd look like a puffball in that huge stadium."

"She'd look fine," I snapped. "They're going to televise it on the stadium giant screen anyhow. It'll be just as easy to see her as to see me. I'm not a giant, you know. They aren't going to be able to see me from the top row."

"What's gotten into you?" asked Cindi.

"I just think it might be better for everybody if it wasn't me," I muttered.

"It has to be you," said Lauren. "The only reason they want us is because of you."

"The only reason they want me is because of my dad, not me," I said angrily. "I don't want to be in the spotlight just 'cause of him. That happens to me all my life, and I'm sick of it."

"I can see where that would be a problem," said Ashley.

"I read about the problems of the sons and daughters of famous people in *People*," said Becky.

"Darlene is not some article in *People* magazine," argued Cindi.

"Stop talking about me in the third person," I said. "I've made up my mind on this. I don't want to do it. I'm going to tell Patrick now. He can get one of you to do it. They'll still want us. It doesn't have to be me."

Cindi grabbed me. "You can't chicken out."

"I'm not chickening out," I said. "I'm just being fair. There's nothing fair about me being front and center. I'm the last one to be front and center. I never win anything."

Cindi stared at me. "What are you talking about?" she asked.

"Even you said it wasn't fair," I said. "I heard you."

"You were in the bathroom!" exclaimed Cindi. "That's what this is about. You heard those two creeps talking about you!"

"Never mind," I said, running out of the locker room. "Just never mind."

Tearing the
Pinecones Apart

I ran into the gym, not really knowing where I wanted to go. I just wanted out of the locker room. Patrick was talking to Jodi's mom. He waved me over to him.

I didn't know what to do. I didn't want to talk to him. I didn't want to talk to anybody. I felt like running away.

Patrick motioned again for me to come talk to him. He looked slightly annoyed that I had ignored him.

I rubbed my eyes. I had no choice.

Slowly I walked over to Patrick.

"Did you do what I asked you to over the weekend?" Patrick asked.

"What's that?" I mumbled. I couldn't remember Patrick asking me anything.

"I asked you to think about what you wanted to do on the beam," said Patrick. "I've hardly thought of anything else. I spent part of the weekend working out what we'll do. I was just explaining it to Sarah. I think we'll start with all of the Pinecones on the beam. Then they'll jump down and look up at you, and the spotlight will focus as you do a pose. Then you'll — "

"Stop right there," I said. "Please — "

Patrick laughed. "No, Darlene. You will definitely not stop right there. I want it to flow from your first pose into a back walkover. You have a very elegant back walkover. Then I thought you'd do a stag leap. I'm looking for moves that will show up well on the screen since very few people will actually be able to see you — "

"Patrick, stop," I begged. "It shouldn't be me. I think you should choreograph a routine for Cindi or Ashley. They're much better than me."

Suddenly the Pinecones came barreling out of the locker room, followed by Ashley and Becky.

"I did *not* say anything wrong." Ashley's high-pitched voice pierced the air.

Lauren, Cindi, and Jodi all flashed Ashley dirty looks when they saw Patrick, me, and Jodi's mom all staring at them.

Cindi ran up to Patrick. "You can't let Darlene

44

back out because of something stupid Ashley said." Cindi was practically screeching.

Patrick looked annoyed. "What is going on here?" he demanded.

I lowered my head. "It's just like I was telling you. I don't want to be the one who does the beam routine. I'll only fall off in front of thousands of people. It'll be too embarrassing. Pick somebody who can really do it."

"But I've just spent the whole weekend talking to the Broncos' staff and planning the program. They want to end the halftime show with a pyramid with your dad and Darryl and Al holding you up. They want to put you at the top of the pyramid."

"That does it. The top of the pyramid is always the smallest person. It should be Ashley."

"Darlene, that's the stupidest thing I've ever heard," argued Lauren. "It's a proven fact that those football players can hold a zebra on top of a pyramid. If they can hold a zebra, they can hold you. You're much smaller than a zebra."

I stared at her. "A zebra? Where did you get that fact?"

"Well, I made that up," Lauren admitted. "It just popped into my mind. But you see what I mean."

"I don't have the foggiest idea what you're talking about," I said. I was getting very confused.

"I know exactly what Lauren means," said Cindi. "Football players are so big they don't care whether it's Darlene or Ashley they hold up, but Darlene's dad sure will care, and so do we."

"But it's still not fair if it's me," I protested. "You even said so."

"I did not," said Cindi, getting red in the face.

"You did, too. I heard you. I'm just trading in on my dad's fame. Everyone always thinks that's what I do."

"Nobody thinks that," said Cindi. "I certainly don't."

"Darlene, you trade on your dad's fame less than anyone I know," said Lauren.

"Who else do you know who has a famous dad?" I asked. I turned to each of them: Cindi, Jodi, and Lauren. "Huh . . . who? Who?"

"Hold it, Darlene. Cool off," said Patrick. "I don't know what you're so riled up about. I don't understand what's going on here."

"They do," I said, nodding my head at my fellow Pinecones. "It just isn't fair that I get to star because I'm my dad's daughter. Ashley said it first, and she's being picked on, but it's not her fault."

Lauren snorted. Ashley gave her a dirty look.

"You're all picking on Ashley and she's only telling the truth," I said.

"Thank you, Darlene," said Ashley. "I don't

think you're mean. I'd never call you Mean Darlene."

I closed my eyes. What a liar!

Patrick put his hand on my arm. "Darlene, if you're serious about wanting to be impartial, it wouldn't be fair if I just picked somebody else. I think that the other Pinecones are right. You're not trading on your father's fame. The only reason the Broncos asked us was because of you. It's an honor for all of us that they want us to take part in their salute to young athletes. You'll disappoint us all if you back out."

"I didn't think of it that way," I admitted.

"Well, I disagree," said Becky. "I think it should be decided the way all things in gymnastics are decided."

"What do you mean?" Cindi asked suspiciously.

"Well, gymnastics is a sport and football is a sport," said Becky. "Darlene's dad, Big Beef, didn't make the team because somebody was being nice to him. He won his spot. It should be the same for whoever gets to star in the halftime show."

"You mean hold a contest?" asked Ashley excitedly.

"Exactly," said Becky.

"Hold it," said Patrick. "Nobody said anything about a contest. Darlene's dad just came and asked for a show featuring Darlene and the Pinecones."

"Well, let it feature the Pinecones," said Becky. "But let the best Pinecone win. The *only* thing to do is hold a contest for the Pinecone who's best on the beam. Don't you think that would be fair, Darlene?" Becky asked me. She was practically taunting me.

"I guess so," I said.

"See?" said Becky. "Darlene wants a contest, Patrick."

"Wait a minute, Becky," said Patrick.

"No, she's right," I said. "It should be a contest."

"What?" exclaimed Cindi.

"I mean it," I said. "I think that a contest is the only fair way to settle this. I definitely won't do it, Patrick, unless you hold a contest."

"Hooray!" said Ashley.

Patrick looked at me. "Are you sure?" he asked.

I nodded. "It should be a contest for all the Pinecones. Maybe you could get a judge to come who doesn't know us. Then it would be fair."

Patrick stroked his chin. "Well, I guess, if that's the way you want it, we could do that. But it's not necessary."

"It's the way I want it," I said.

The other Pinecones looked at me as if I had gone off the deep end.

"You make me so mad," whispered Cindi. "You shouldn't have done that."

I stared at her. "I thought you'd be happy," I said. "Now you have a chance to be the one in the spotlight. I did it for the good of the Pinecones."

Cindi looked skeptical. "How can it be for the good of the Pinecones? We were just fine. Now we have to compete against each other, and you've given that creep Ashley a chance to be the star. Why didn't you at least talk it over with us?"

"I didn't think," I admitted.

"Why did you have to give in to Ashley and Becky?" Cindi demanded.

I looked over at Ashley and Becky. Ashley looked triumphant, as if she already knew that she was the winner.

"How do you think the Pinecones are gonna feel if that little pipsqueak represents us?" Cindi asked.

Cindi turned away from me. I was feeling shaky inside. I couldn't believe what I had done. What had I gotten myself into? Was I going to wind up tearing the Pinecones apart?

Not Everybody Can Be at the Top

Dad was waiting for me outside. Monday is his day off. It's the only day that he can pick me up.

I've never gotten used to seeing my dad in pain. I should have. Every Monday he can barely get out of bed. He spends most of the day applying ice bags to the different parts of his body that hurt.

But still, he had gotten himself tucked into his sports car to pick me up after practice. Usually I love it when Daddy comes to get me by himself.

I slipped in beside him. I could see that the right side of his face was swollen where the defensive lineman had tried to rip his face mask off. His whole cheek was swollen from the bruise.

He smiled at me.

"How's the gymnast?" he asked.

"Not so great," I mumbled. "How are you feeling?"

"Not so great myself," said Dad, and he laughed. "Where are you hurting? Shinsplints again?"

"No." A lot of the time I did get shinsplints from vaulting.

"It's funny," said Dad. "I've felt a lot closer to you since you've been taking gymnastics."

"You mean 'cause now I sometimes hurt, too?" I said.

Dad glanced over at me. "No, I don't like to see you aching. I never wanted to push you into sports, but I'm glad you found one that you love."

I didn't answer.

Dad put the car in gear, but he didn't go. He opened the window and waved hello to Cindi, Lauren, and Jodi.

"Hi ya, Pinecones," he said.

"Dad, let's go," I said.

"What's the hurry?" he answered. "I was just saying hello to the gang."

"We're not a gang," I said. "We're just four kids who were thrown together because we started Patrick's at the same time. Can we please get out of here?"

Cindi, Lauren, and Jodi were in a tight circle whispering together and looking at me. I couldn't get over the fact that Cindi was mad at me. I felt like I had just made a big mess out of everything. All I wanted to do was disappear for a while.

"Dad, please," I urged. "Can we get out of here?"

"I don't get it," said Dad as we drove away. "I thought the four of you were a team."

"Gymnastics is an individual sport, Dad," I said, sinking down into the leather seat. I turned on the tape deck, loud.

Dad didn't say anything. I wasn't paying any attention to where we were going. Maybe I shouldn't have let Ashley and Becky goad me into making it into a contest, but did Cindi have to get mad at me?

I looked up. We were at the entrance to the freeway.

"Which way?" asked Dad.

Which-way is the name of the game that my dad and I play. The person in the passenger seat gets to tell the driver which way to go. Ordinarily I love to try to get him lost.

"Which way?" Dad asked again.

"I don't care," I said.

"I don't care is not in the rules of which-way," said Dad.

52

"I'm not in the mood for a game, Dad," I answered.

"I don't think I can play which-way by myself," said Dad. "But I'll try."

Dad turned the car onto the freeway leading to downtown Denver, away from our house.

"Daddy!" I cried. "I want to go home. I don't want to play which-way."

"Too late," said Dad. "I can't jump off the freeway. Besides, you and I haven't played this in a long time."

"I'm too old for this game."

"You're never too old for which-way," said Dad.

We sped along the freeway past several green exit signs. "Which way?" Dad asked.

I pointed to the next exit.

Dad steered the car down the ramp. I hadn't realized what exit I had pointed to. Mile High Stadium loomed up in front of us.

"Taking me back to the scene of yesterday's crime?" asked Dad. The Broncos had lost.

"I didn't realize this was the exit I chose," I admitted with a sort of silly grin. It was incredible. Maybe some ESP had led me here. Dad and I hadn't taken a which-way ride in months and then I direct him right to Mile High Stadium — the place where I would have been center stage if I hadn't fouled everything up.

It's called Mile High Stadium because Denver

is a mile high above sea level. On a Sunday when the Broncos are playing, you can't get a car near the place. Now it looked practically deserted.

The guard waved Dad through to the players' parking lot. Almost all the players had Monday off. The next day the team would be looking at the game films of Sunday's loss.

"Why are we parking?" I asked. "I don't want to get out. Dad, I'm really not in the mood to see anybody."

"Who said anything about seeing anybody?" Dad asked. "Let's just take a walk. It'll be private in there."

I crossed my arms over my chest.

"Come on, Darlene," said Dad. "Something's obviously bothering you. And this is the quietest place I know. Let's stretch our legs. It'll be good for us both."

I followed Dad through the maze of tunnels underneath the stadium.

The coaches were previewing the films of Sunday's game. The coach of the offensive line looked worried when he saw Dad.

He left the film room and came out into the corridor. "Beef? What are you doing here? Are you hurt?"

"No," said Dad. "Just a few bruises. I'm fine. Darlene and I just ended up near the stadium and took a walk."

"Darlene, did you come to practice?" asked the coach. "You're going to be one of the kids in the halftime show, aren't you?"

"Sure she is," said Dad. "I just picked her up from gymnastics."

"Are you nervous?" asked the coach.

"Sort of," I mumbled.

Dad looked at me. He put his huge hand around my shoulder. "We'll see you later," he said to his coach.

We walked out onto the football field. After the game, the field looked like it had been attacked by a plague of gophers. The grass was all pitted and dug up. Dad loves playing on real grass. He says that his career would have been cut short long ago if he had to play on artificial turf. Most of the stadiums that he plays in when he's out of town have AstroTurf, and Dad hates it. A normal tackle leaves him with deep bruises.

I followed Dad as he climbed into the stands. We were the only spectators among 75,000 empty seats. Mile High Stadium is a huge horse-shoe with each section painted a different color: blue, yellow, orange, and red.

I had been here plenty of times to see Dad play, but I had never been in it empty like this. I looked down at the grass where they were going to set up a beam.

I would probably have looked like a flea in a flea circus.

"Okay, spill the beans," said Dad, leaning back with his elbows on the bench in back of him.

"What beans?" I asked.

"What's going on?" asked Dad.

"Nothing," I mumbled.

"Darlene, one thing I love about you is that you never can hide your feelings. Are you mad at me for something? Are you getting cold feet about the halftime show? I did kind of spring it on you."

"I'm not mad at you," I said.

"Are you mad at the Pinecones?" Dad asked. "It wasn't like you not to want to stop and talk to them."

"No . . . they're mad at me, at least I think they are. It's just a big mess. Everyone thinks it's unfair that I'm going to star in the halftime show." I knew I was exaggerating here. I wasn't sure that everyone thought that.

"But the Broncos wanted my daughter," Dad said. "They want as many children of the players as they can get."

"I'll still come out with the others, but maybe I won't be the star."

"What does that mean?" asked Dad. "Maybe? How maybe?"

I stared at the football field and at the stands

across the field. "Dad, I would have been too nervous to do my beam routine out there anyhow. What if I did nothing but fall off? It'll be much better to have the best person from the Pinecones be on the beam. I'd die in front of thousands of screaming people."

"Sometimes being in front of thousands of people all screaming *for* you is fun," said Dad.

"Well, I'll never know," I said. "We decided to make it a contest. We're going to have a little in-club meet, and I'm sure someone else will win. Probably Ashley or Cindi. They're best on the beam."

Dad looked thoughtful. "When did all this come about?"

"Just today," I said. "Patrick is going to get a judge. It'll just be a one-event contest for the Pinecones."

"Are you at least going to try to win?" Dad asked.

"Of course, I'll try," I said, but I wouldn't look at my dad. I'd try, but I wouldn't win. Right now I felt so mixed up I wasn't even sure I wanted to win.

Dad leaned over and held me tight. He gave me a big hug and a kiss. Then he stood up and took my hand said, "Come on. Follow me."

We climbed down the stands and onto the field.

"Do a back flip," he said.

"Dad."

"Just do it. There's nobody here, except me."

I took a few running steps and then did a roundoff and back flip.

I was breathing hard when I finished.

"Was that fun?" Dad asked.

I nodded. "When I do a tumbling run, or finally get a new trick in gymnastics, I feel like I'm a firecracker. It's just so much fun."

"You know the reason I play football?" he asked.

"So you can drive a red Jaguar?" I teased.

Dad shook his head. "I do it because it's still fun. It's the only reason to do it. Otherwise it's too painful."

"Gymnastics can be pretty painful, too," I said, thinking about the way my stomach always felt after I'd been working out on the bars, or my shins felt after vaulting.

"Darlene, honey," said Dad. "I love watching you do gymnastics because it's given you grace and strength, but I love it the most because I've seen you feel a part of a team. Don't throw that away because you're scared."

"But, Dad," I protested. "I thought I had done something that would be good for the team, by giving everybody a chance."

"But?" asked Dad.

"Cindi said that I had just made things worse.

That they were happy with the way things were. But I can't go to Patrick now and say that I changed my mind — that there shouldn't be a contest. That wouldn't be fair, either."

"I agree," said Dad. "So it seems like you've only got one choice."

"What's that?" I asked.

"To try to win that contest," said Dad.

"I don't have a chance," I said.

"You don't if you say that. You'll never win if you have that attitude. You've got to go in with the attitude that you're going to win. Winners are people who have a winning attitude. If you go in saying you won't have a chance, you won't have a chance. Believe me, Darlene. I know."

"You always told me that winning wasn't everything."

"*Wanting* to win is," said Dad.

"Even if I don't win, I'll still be there with the other Pinecones."

"But I wanted to see you on the top. I wanted the chance to hold you on my shoulders above the crowd."

"Not everybody can be on the top, Dad," I argued.

"Exactly," said Dad. "Exactly."

9

There's Such a Thing as Being Too Fair

"Where were you two?" asked Mom when we got back. "The phone's been ringing off the hook."

"Was it reporters wanting to know if I survived yesterday?" Dad asked. He picked up Debi and gave her a hug.

Mom shook her head. "No, the Pinecones have been calling for Darlene, one after another. Jodi says that it's urgent you call her back. So does Cindi, and so does Lauren. They all say to call Jodi."

"I'll do it later."

"You'd better do it now," said Dad.

"Jodi did say there was something they had to talk to you about right away," said Mom.

Now, why do those words always sound so scary? Those must be the scariest words in the English language. No one ever says, "I want to talk to you," if they've got something good to say.

"Call Jodi now, " suggested Dad. "Don't put them off. That's no way to treat friends."

"But, but . . . " I started to stammer. And then I stopped. Dad was right.

Jodi answered the phone on the first ring.

"It's me, Darlene," I said.

"The Pinecone Brigade summons you to a meeting," said Jodi.

"Is this a court-martial?" I asked, trying to joke, but I wasn't sure I was kidding.

"Just get over here," said Jodi. "Can you come over right now? We want to talk to you. Cindi and Lauren are already here."

"Hold on a second," I said. I put my hand over the receiver. "Can I go over to Jodi's?"

"I don't know, Darlene," said my mom. "Do you have homework?"

Dad looked at me. "Let her go," he said. "I think it's important."

"Jodi, I'll be right there," I said. "But can you tell me what it's about?"

"We'll talk about it when you get here," she said. "Put on your leotard and your gymnastics shoes."

"Why?" I exclaimed.

"Just do it. We want you dressed for action. And hurry!" Jodi sounded like a drill sergeant.

I went up to my room. Did the Pinecones think I wasn't one of them anymore? Did they think I was too much of a coward for giving in to Ashley and Becky?

I opened my drawer and pulled out a leotard with a rainbow on it. Then I put on my old gymnastic slippers.

At least if it was a mock court-martial, I'd look good. Dad drove me over to Jodi's. I didn't talk much. I was too scared. Dad knew it. He gave me a hug as I got out of the car. "Remember," he said. "Think like a winner."

"How will that help if my friends are mad at me?" I asked.

"You don't know what's going on in there," said Dad. "It could be something completely different than you expect."

"Yeah, it could be something much worse," I said, getting out of the car.

"Just don't think of yourself as a loser," Dad warned. "You aren't."

I rang the doorbell. Jodi's mom opened the door. "Hi, Darlene. The kids are waiting for you in Jodi's room," she said. She sounded as if she almost felt sorry for me.

I knocked on the door timidly.

"Come in," said Jodi.

I walked into Jodi's room, which is tiny. All three of the Pinecones were standing on her low beam, which sits a few inches off the floor. As soon as I walked in, they started rapping, "DARLENE—NOT—MEAN—DARLENE—SHE'S KEEN — DARLENE FOR QUEEN. . . . "

Jodi took out a peice of paper and read, "There once was a girl named Darlene — "

"She didn't know how to be mean," said Lauren and Cindi like they were a rap chorus.

"She got the jitters . . . she almost turned into fritters."

"Darlene was a girl who needed some help," read Jodi.

"Without the Pinecones she would have turned into kelp," rapped Lauren.

"Kelp?" I asked.

"We couldn't think of anything else that rhymed with help," said Lauren. "Anyhow, shut up a second. We've got to finish our rap."

"I've never seen three whiter rappers," I said.

"Hush up," said Cindi.

Then my Pinecones did their final verse.

"The Pinecones want Darlene to be a star."

"If Ashley wins the contest, she won't go far."

Then they repeated the DARLENE — NOT MEAN verse.

I fell onto the bed. Dad had said it might be something I didn't expect. But I couldn't believe it. I was so relieved I felt like crying.

"What was that about?" I asked. "I don't get it. I thought you were mad at me."

"We were," said Cindi. "We thought you should have talked to us before you let Ashley and Becky push you into making it into a contest."

"Then Cindi told us about Ashley calling you 'Mean Darlene,' " said Lauren. "I wish I had been there. I would have punched her clock."

"We decided we can't let her get away with it," said Jodi.

"We tried to get you, but no one knew where you were."

"I was with my dad," I said. "We wound up at the stadium. I saw where we'll perform."

"The only one who should star at the halftime show is *you*," said Cindi. "We're not gonna compete against you."

"But that's ridiculous!" I was almost shouting. "That won't be fair. Besides, Ashley will never drop out, and that just means that she'll win."

"I can't stand your attitude!" cried Cindi. "Can't you think of yourself as a winner, just once? You'll never be a winner if you don't think like one."

"That's exactly what my father says," I admitted.

64

"We want you to win back the chance to star in the halftime show," said Jodi.

"We're all going to work together and choreograph an incredible routine for you to do on the beam," said Lauren.

"We've been working on it all afternoon," said Jodi.

"Wait a minute, wait a minute," I said. "You all would have had as much of a chance as me to be the star. Why help me?"

" 'Cause this whole thing was getting out of hand," said Cindi. "You're the one who is Big Beef's daughter. It should never have been made into a contest. But you let it happen, and we can't let Ashley and Becky think they've outsmarted a Pinecone."

"That would be a disgrace worse than death," said Lauren.

"That might be going a little bit too far," said Jodi.

"It doesn't feel right," I protested.

"Don't worry," said Lauren. "The next time we compete against you, we'll try to beat the pants off you."

"But if you drop out, Ashley will just work all the harder. There's no guarantee that I'll win."

"Now this is the secret part of our plan," said Lauren. "We aren't going to back out until the last minute. That way Ashley will sort of be lulled into thinking that you're not her only competition. If she knows we're helping you, she'll just try to do even harder tricks."

"That's very sneaky," I said.

"That's why we like it, " said Jodi.

"We've got two new tricks we want you to learn. They're not too hard. I showed them to Mom and she said they were tricks that a gymnast as good as you could learn on her own. Luckily you've got a beam a home, and I have this one. Ashley won't even know what you've got in store for her."

"Now, get up here on the beam," said Cindi. "Let us show you what we've got in mind for you."

I stepped onto the beam. "But are you sure this is fair?" I asked. "It's sort of a sneaky trick to play on Ashley."

Cindi put her hands on her hips. "There is such a thing as being too fair, you know," she said.

10

Maybe the Best Person Will Win

My stomach muscles were so sore from the night before that it hurt to roll over in bed. I knew this must be how my dad felt on Monday mornings. I had been working all night on the routine that the Pinecones had choreographed for me.

They had planned a very weird way to start my routine. It was called a "chest-stand mount." It certainly would surprise Ashley. Jodi got it out of one of her mother's books. I put my chest on the beam and pull my feet straight into the air so that I'm upside down. It's easier than a hand-stand mount, but it's still pretty hard. If I did it wrong I'd look like a fool because I could fall right on my nose. I practiced it on the low beam and it wasn't scary because my nose was just inches from the floor, and Cindi and Jodi were holding me up. But who knew what would happen when I tried it on the high beam without the Pinecones spotting me?

It's hard to picture. It's even harder to do. But I had to admit if I could learn to do it without help, it would impress the judge, bang! right from the start. On the other hand, if I did it wrong, I would land on my nose right at the judge's feet.

I rolled out of bed and into the shower. The hot water felt good. When I went down to breakfast, Baby Deirdre was already in her high chair, and Debi was sitting at the table. Mom was making eggs. Deirdre was banging her spoon on her tray. I couldn't stand the noise. I took the spoon away from her, and she started to cry.

"Why did you do that?" Debi asked. "She wants her spoon."

"It was making too much noise," I said. "It'll wake up Dad."

"Dad's already awake," said Debi. "You did it just to be mean."

"Mean," repeated Deirdre.

Debi giggled. "Mean Darlene." Debi tried to teach Deirdre. She leaned over and repeated the words into Deirdre's ear.

"Cut that out," I said. I didn't need anybody to

68

remind me about "Mean Darlene." I just wanted some peace and quiet.

"Debi and Darlene, stop fighting," said my mom.

"Darlene is mean," said Debi. "She woke up like Oscar the Grouch this morning."

"You did seem to get up on the wrong side of the bed this morning," said my mother.

"How can she get out on the wrong side?" Debi asked. "One side of her bed is against the wall."

"It's just an expression, dumb-face," I said to my sister.

"She called me dumb-face," said Debi.

Mom put a plate of eggs in front of me. "Apologize to your sister," she said.

"I'm sorry, " I said, but I didn't mean it. Mom was right. I was in a lousy mood.

Mom sat down with us. "What's wrong this morning, Darlene? Did you have a bad time over at Jodi's last night? You stayed long enough."

"No. The Pinecones were terrific to me," I said. "Almost too good. Mom, can you keep a secret?"

Mom smiled at me.

I told her what the Pinecones were doing for me.

"I don't get it," said Mom. "I thought it was all set that you were going to star in the halftime show on the beam."

"Some of the kids didn't think it was fair," I explained.

"But not the Pinecones?" asked Mom.

"Not the original Pinecones. But this new girl, Ashley. She's better than us at most things, but she hasn't worked on the beam much. Patrick's put her with us. She's the one who wants to star in the halftime show."

"You're wonderful on the beam," said Mom. "I love to watch you. I bet you can beat her."

"Yeah, but Ashley is a *really* good gymnast," I said. "She's an unbelievable tumbler and vaulter. She's gonna be great on the beam. See, if the other Pinecones drop out," I explained to Mom, "it's really down to a contest between this little kid and me."

"How little?" asked Debi. "As little as me?"

"No, but she's as much of a pain in the neck."

"Darlene," said my mother. "I know you're upset about this, but don't take it out on everyone around here."

"Sorry," I said again to Debi.

"Maybe I'll vote for the other girl to win your contest," said Debi.

"You don't vote for someone. It's not a popularity contest. I'm gonna be judged."

"Is that what's worrying you?" Mom asked. "Sometimes I know you don't like pressure. Maybe that's why you're scared."

I took a bite of egg. "I thought I was making things easier when I told Patrick that the best person should win and get to be the star."

"Sweetheart, you know you have a chance. I think the best person will win, and it'll be you."

"But, Mom," I protested. "Now if I don't win, I'll have let down all the Pinecones, too. "

"Then you'll just have to win," said Mom.

That afternoon, the Pinecones insisted on coming over to my house to work on the rest of my routine.

"I'm still sore from last night," I complained.

"No pain . . . no gain," said Jodi.

Debi was downstairs in the gym/playroom practicing tiptoeing across the low beam. She's going to start gymnastics next year, and I bet she'll be really good.

"I need the beam," I told her.

"I'm practicing," she said.

I picked Debi up and plunked her on the couch. "Practice being a couch potato," I said. "I've got serious stuff to practice."

"Right, Debi," said Cindi. "Don't you want Darlene to be a winner?"

"I want to be a winner," said Debi.

"That's the spirit," said Lauren. She turned to me. "That little kid is gonna be a terror."

"I know," I agreed. "Maybe she'll be able to beat Ashley someday."

"No cop-outs," said Cindi. "*You're* the one who's going to beat Ashley."

"Let's get to work," said Jodi. She brought out a gymnastics book with pictures: *Gymnastics for Girls* by Dr. Frank Ryan.

"We want you to do something that Patrick hasn't taught us," said Jodi. "It's called a forward Tinsica, and it starts like a cartwheel and then twists into a front walkover."

"It sounds impossible," I said.

Debi giggled.

"It's going to be great for you," said Cindi. "You've got a beautiful cartwheel, and a great front walkover. You'll look good doing it because your legs are so long. I checked it out with my mom. She says you're up to it."

"Does she know what we're doing?" I asked.

"I swore her to secrecy," said Jodi. "But I didn't want to try to teach you something if you could end up hurting yourself."

"She said I could do this?" I exclaimed, studying the book.

Jodi nodded. "See, you end the trick in a beautiful pose. One hand is in the air. You'll look beautiful. It'll knock their socks off."

"It looks like it'll knock me off," I said, studying the pictures.

"Come on," said Lauren. "Try it on the low beam. We'll spot you."

I tried it. Jodi held on to my waist, and Lauren stood on a chair and grabbed my feet at the top of the cartwheel to help me get the twist. Cindi guided my hands.

"Great," said Jodi.

"Yeah, it only took three of you holding me up to do it," I said. "I'll never learn to do this by myself."

"Never say never," said Lauren.

"Wait till you do it a hundred times," said Cindi. "You'll master it."

I groaned. It suddenly dawned on me. The Pinecone Brigade might turn out to be the toughest coaches in town.

"I want to do that trick," said Debi.

I wiped the sweat from my forehead. "No way, baby sister. This is my show."

"It's not fair," said Debi, and she flounced out of the room.

Cindi laughed. "No offense, but she sounds like a miniature Ashley. 'It's not fair' are Ashley's favorite words."

Ashley! Why did they have to mention Ashley?

I got back on the beam to try the trick again. This was gonna be murder.

11

I Only Work
With Winners!

Patrick announced that he had found a judge to come in a week from Monday.

"That only gives me a few more days to get ready," I exclaimed. "I'll never get it by then."

"What about the rest of you?" Patrick asked Cindi, Jodi, and Lauren. "I haven't seen you working on your beam routines."

Lauren giggled. "Don't worry about us," she said.

Patrick looked at her suspiciously.

"What's going on?" he asked.

"Nothing," said Lauren, giggling.

We all went into the locker room. Suddenly Becky grabbed me. "I've been hearing rumors," she said. "Rumors about you and the Pine-cones." Cindi, Lauren, and Jodi turned around.

"What's that?" I asked.

"Some kind of secret plan you're trying to pull. You've got something sneaky up your sleeve."

"That's ridiculous," I said.

"Well, I heard it from a reliable source." Becky was practically sneering at me.

I wondered who it could have been. Jodi, Cindi, Lauren and I all stared at each other. I was sure none of us had told anybody what we were doing.

"So who was this 'reliable source'?" I asked Becky. I could tell she was dying to tell me. Becky is such a gossip that she can't stand keeping anything to herself.

"It comes from someone very close to you," Becky whispered.

"Becky, just come out with it," I said. "Besides," I added quickly. "There really isn't anything going on."

"That's not what your little sister Debi says," taunted Becky.

"Debi!" I exclaimed. "She's not even in kindergarten. How do you know her?"

"She goes to the same nursery school as my little sister," said Becky. "She came over to my house to play yesterday. When I told her I went to Patrick's with you, she said, "Oh, Darlene's gonna win that contest to be in my dad's halftime show." Becky was a great mimic. She sounded exactly like Debi's little girl voice.

"Debi always thinks I'm going to win," I said, thinking quickly. "She thinks winning is something that people vote on. Don't pay any attention to her."

"Then Debi said *all* the Pinecones were helping you," said Becky, suspiciously. She scowled at Cindi, Lauren, and Jodi.

"We help each other," I said. "We always have."

"Yeah," echoed Lauren.

"Who's helping Ashley?" Becky asked.

"Right," piped up Ashley. "Who's helping me?"

I shrugged. "I don't know."

"Debi said you were learning a new trick," Becky said.

I was going to have to kill my little sister.

"She called it a toupee," said Becky.

"Oh, yeah, that's the trick where Darlene does a cartwheel and her wig falls off," said Lauren. "You know how much Darlene loves to change her hair styles? We got her a bunch of wigs. The toupee is great. You'll probably see it in the Olympics soon."

"Well," said Becky. "I decided to help Ashley. I just think it will look better for Patrick's club if someone really good and cute gets to represent us."

Lauren rolled her eyes. "You are such a wonderful person. Always thinking of the good of the group. But don't try to teach Ashley the toupee. It's too hard for her."

"Nothing's too hard for me," bragged Ashley. "I want to learn the toupee. Can't you teach it to me, Becky?"

We all started laughing. "Yeah, Becky. I'm sure you know how to teach Ashley the toupee. Ashley will look great in a toupee."

"At least she's petite and cute," said Becky. "Ashley looks like a gymnast."

"Darlene is both good and cute," said Jodi.

"Cute," I said, looking down at my big feet. "No one has ever called me cute."

"Well, Patrick is not going to think you're cute," said Becky. "Your little sister Debi didn't get everything wrong. She also said the other Pinecones were going to drop out at the last minute to make sure that you won."

"*I'm* gonna strangle your little sister," muttered Cindi.

"Darlene?" asked Becky. "Is your little sister a liar or is she telling the truth?"

I swallowed hard. I turned my back on Becky and spoke to Cindi, Lauren, and Jodi. "We've got to tell Patrick now," I said. "It's not fair to him."

"I'm waiting for an answer," said Becky.

"Come on, guys," I pleaded. "Our cover's blown. We've got to go to Patrick. It really isn't fair to do it the way we planned. We'd be making a fool out of him."

Lauren groaned. "I hate that 'fair' word," she said. "But Darlene's got a point. I think we should go talk to Patrick before Becky does."

"And tell him what?" sneered Becky. "That you three little cowards were trying to rig it so Darlene would win?"

"Go stuff your mouth with your size-four slipper," I said.

I slammed open the swinging door from the locker room to the gym. "Patrick!" I shouted. "We've got to talk to you."

Patrick looked up. "Now what?" he asked.

"It's about the contest," I said.

Patrick groaned. "I can't change the date. It's the only date that my friend can do it. You'll have to be ready."

"No, it's not about the date," I said.

"What is going on?" Patrick demanded.

Lauren sighed. "Well, Cindi, Jodi, and I don't want to compete against Darlene. I mean, it's not like it's a real meet. We'd compete against her then. But this doesn't feel right."

"We decided we won't compete," said Jodi.

"Becky was right! Becky was right!" sang Ashley. "They were planning something very sneaky."

"It wasn't sneaky. This was never supposed to have been a contest in the first place," Cindi practically shouted at her.

"Cindi," said Patrick sharply. "Let's straighten this out without shouting."

"Darlene said she'd let it be a contest," whined Ashley. "Didn't you?"

"Yes," I admitted.

"If they drop out, then it's just between you and me!" cried Ashley, as if it were just now dawning on her. She sounded very pleased about it. "I can beat you," Ashley blurted out.

Patrick looked at me. "The whole idea of making it a contest for who gets to star in the half-time show was your idea, not mine, Darlene," he said.

"I know," I admitted. "Will your friend still come to judge even if it's just between Ashley and me?" I was kind of hoping he would say no.

"I don't see why he should mind," said Patrick. "It'll just make it easier for him."

"Then it's settled," I said.

"I'm glad Becky's helping me," said Ashley. "With Becky helping me, I can't lose."

"Come on, Ashley," said Becky. "We'll work on your routine right now."

Becky put her arm around Ashley. "I only work with winners," she said over her shoulder. She paused as if she had something more to say. Then she seemed to change her mind.

She didn't have to say it. I knew what she was thinking. If Ashley was a winner, I was a loser.

My Toupee Fell Off

It was the Sunday before the contest. All the
Pinecones were over at my house. I was glad my
dad was playing an away game. We had taken
over the weight room for the entire weekend.

I was sweating.

"Try it again," Cindi insisted.

I hopped back onto the beam.

"I think the secret is opening your legs as wide
as you can at the top of the cartwheel," said Jodi,
studying her book.

I tried the Tinsica, or toupee as we had taken
to calling it, one more time. I almost got it, but
at the last minute I lost my balance and had to
jump off the beam.

"I think the secret is to cut that trick out of

81

my routine," I said. "I'll only foul it up."

"You've done it in practice," argued Lauren.

"Yeah, I've done it successfully about three times. You know under pressure I'll never be able to do it."

I took off the rubber band I had been using to pull my hair back. "I'm sunk. Ashley is going to win for sure."

"Don't you dare say that," said Cindi, almost angrily. "You're better than Ashley. You're better than Becky."

"Right," said Lauren. "And if we keep in your spectacular toupee trick, you can't lose."

"I'm not joking," I said. "Ashley's going to beat the pants off me. You know, she's really a better gymnast."

Jodi took me by the shoulders. "Stop thinking like that. You've got to think like a winner."

"Thinking isn't going to make me a winner," I said. "I'm being objective. Ashley really is better."

"She's gonna win for sure if you have that attitude," said Lauren.

"You guys have been terrific," I said. "But we can't do the impossible."

Cindi looked disgusted. "What are we going to do with her?" she exclaimed to the others.

"Look," I said. "I've heard all those lectures about having a winning attitude. All the words in the world won't help me do the Tinsica."

"She's right," said Lauren.

"Thank you," I said, lying down on the mat. I was exhausted. "I'm glad we've got at least one realist here."

"You've got to *see* yourself as a winner," said Lauren. "We've been going about it in the wrong way. Close your eyes."

"Gladly," I said. I closed my eyes.

"Cross your arms over your chest and close your eyes."

"Is this creative rest?" Jodi asked.

"I'm gonna try something by Joe Massimo I read once in a gymnastics magazine," said Lauren.

"How does she remember everything she reads?" asked Jodi.

"She's got a photographic memory," said Cindi. "Shut up, and let Lauren try it. We've tried everything else."

"Darlene, you're going to the movies," said Lauren. "Make a big, white movie screen in your mind. Breathe deeply. And don't talk to me. Let me do the talking."

I took a deep breath and I tried to picture a white screen. It was hard to keep it there. I kept getting other colors, muddy pinks and blues, but the more I breathed in and out, the whiter the screen got.

"Now picture a red dot in the middle of the screen," said Lauren. "And let it grow."

As the red dot started to grow, I could feel my breaths getting deeper and deeper. "Now shrink the color back to a red dot and make the screen empty again," commanded Lauren. "Picture yourself in the gym. Go over to the beam and stand next to it."

I took a deep breath.

"Salute the judge," said Lauren. "You are so strong. Now start doing your routine."

I pictured myself doing my whole routine perfectly and then I started laughing.

I opened my eyes. "Why are you laughing?" Lauren asked.

"My toupee fell off," I said, rolling on the floor.

"Very funny," said Lauren. "Did it work?"

I shrugged. "I don't know. I did get a movie screen in my mind."

"Come on," said Cindi. "Get on the beam and try it."

I stood on the beam with one leg extended and my arms over my head.

I took a deep breath the way I had when I was lying on the floor.

Then I lunged and began the trick. My feet found the beam again as I arched my back and I pulled myself up into the final pose.

The Pinecones all burst into cheers.

"You did it!" Cindi exclaimed. "Now just do it like that again tomorrow. It was perfect."

Doing it at home with my friends was one thing. But doing it in front of a judge would be something else. Practice doesn't count. Winning does.

13

It's a Toss-up

"I can't believe this whole thing was my idea in the first place," I moaned.

It was time for the contest. I was so nervous I could barely talk. Patrick's friend, the judge, was in the gym. Patrick had told us to get ready. It was all too informal, not at all like a regular meet. In a regular meet, all the other Pinecones would be nervous, too. The locker room would be full of girls looking scared.

Here I was, the only one who looked like she wanted to throw up. Ashley was already in the gym, warming up. There was no audience, no parents — just the two of us. Patrick was acting like it was no big deal. But it was to me.

"Have you been practicing my mental imaging?" Lauren asked.

"I tried," I said. "Last night before I went to sleep, I made my mind a movie screen. Then I tried to do my routine. Only I fell off."

Lauren looked horrified.

"That's good, that's good," said Jodi quickly. "It's okay that Darlene practiced falling off in her mind. That's how she'll overcome her fear."

"Thanks, Jodi," I said. I knew she was only saying that to make me feel better. "But what if I fall off for real, not in the movies?"

"You'll do what all great gymnasts do," said Jodi.

"And what is that?" I asked.

"Remount," said Jodi. "Get right back on the beam and finish your routine. That's what my sister and Mom always tell me to do when I fall off the beam."

"Jodi's right," said Cindi. "Suppose you do fall off. It doesn't mean you've lost. You've got to think like a winner. Attack the beam."

"Think like a winner," I repeated. "I'll try."

Cindi grabbed my arm. "Nobody can *try* to think like a winner. You've just got to do it, Darlene. Say to yourself, 'I'm gonna win.'"

"That sounds like I'm bragging."

"If you don't say it, the Pinecones are going to sit on you," said Jodi.

"Okay, okay," I said. "I am a winner." I said the words softly.

"Louder," said Cindi.

"I am a winner!" I said. I felt silly. It sounded like something from a *Rocky* movie. But I said it. "I am a winner."

I walked out into the gym. Cindi, Lauren, and Jodi followed behind me, like I was a prize fighter and they were my seconds.

Ashley was already waiting for us with Becky and her friends surrounding her.

Patrick was talking to his friend.

He introduced Ashley and me.

"This is going to be a most unusual event," said Patrick. "We only have two girls competing. They've both prepared an optional beam routine by themselves. I want to say that I'm very proud of the two girls who have stayed in the competition. I know you've both worked very hard by yourselves to work out your own routines."

I coughed.

Cindi clapped me on the back. I hadn't exactly worked totally by myself.

Then I saw Becky whispering in Ashley's ear. Ashley had gotten help, too.

Patrick took a coin out of his pocket. "Since there are only the two of you, we'll toss to see who goes first."

He turned to me and Ashley. "Which of you wants to call it?" he asked.

"You can do it," I said to Ashley.

"Stop being so nice," Lauren whispered to me. But it was too late. Patrick had already flipped the coin high into the air.

"Heads," shouted Ashley.

The coin turned over and over in the air. I watched it drop down onto the blue mat.

Patrick leaned over it. "Tails," he said. "Darlene, it's your choice."

"I'll go first," I started to say, but before I could finish the sentence I saw Cindi waving her hands in the air.

"No," said Jodi. She grabbed my arm and pulled me away. "One second," Jodi said, as she dragged me to a corner of the gym. The other Pinecones huddled around me. "Take last," said Jodi.

"I want to get it over with," I said. "I'll feel much more relaxed if I go first. I'm so nervous, I'm gonna die."

"But the judge is used to looking for the best to go last," argued Jodi. "Ashley's nervous, too."

I glanced over at her. She was stretching out on the mats, doing an incredible split.

"She doesn't look nervous," I said.

"She's just trying to psych you out," said

Cindi. "You've got to psych *her* out. Go last."

"Why did I ever let myself into this?" I groaned.

"It's too late to back out now," said Lauren, pushing me back toward Patrick.

"I'll go last," I said.

Ashley's head jerked up. She looked shocked. She glanced at Becky. Becky shrugged. I was sure Becky had told Ashley that I'd want to go first.

Now I was glad I had won the toss.

Now I was glad that I was going last. Let Ashley worry for a change.

Fair and Square

Patrick set up a folding table near the beam. He put a bell on it. Then he pulled up a folding chair for the judge.

"I'll be the official timer," said Patrick. "You'll have a maximum time of one minute and fifteen seconds to complete your routines. I'll ring the bell when it's fifteen seconds before the end. If you fall, you have thirty seconds to remount, and those seconds are not deducted from your total time on the beam. Any questions?"

"Just one," said Becky.

Patrick looked annoyed. "Becky, you're not even one of the contestants."

"I'm an honorary coach for Ashley," said Becky.

"All right," said Patrick. "What's your question?"

"Before I let Ashley start, I want the other Pinecones to promise that they'll stick with the judge's decision," she said.

"What does that mean?" I asked angrily.

"Well, Darlene," said Becky sweetly, "it seems to me that you've been all over the place about this halftime show. First, you were supposed to star because it was *your* father. Then you decided to have a contest. Then your friends dropped out. I just don't want little Ashley to compete if you've got it rigged. What if she wins, and then you decide you want to star?"

"I wouldn't do that!" I was so mad I was practically sputtering. "I wouldn't go back on my word."

Cindi, Lauren, and Jodi practically had to hold me back. "She's just saying that so you'll lose your concentration," whispered Lauren.

"Becky," said Patrick. "That was uncalled for."

"I just want to hear from Darlene that if the best person wins, the best person will get to be the star at the halftime show."

"You've got my word," I muttered.

"What's that?" Becky asked.

"I give you my word," I said, enunciating every syllable.

"Okay," said Becky, smiling. She knew she had

92

gotten my goat. I felt like my head was spinning.

"All right," said Patrick. "Enough of this nonsense. Ashley, are you ready?"

Ashley nodded. She stood at the end of the beam and put the springboard about a foot away from the beam. She saluted the judge with a big grin on her face. She looked just adorable.

Then she ran up to the springboard and did a one-legged leap onto the beam. It was a very risky approach because it's so easy to fall off, but she held her balance and ended in a beautiful pose with one leg lifted high and her toe perfectly pointed.

I could tell she was relieved she had made it. Then she did a little waltz across the beam. I could see her counting off the waltz steps to herself. Becky had been smart choreographing her routine. There was something so charming about seeing a little sprite like Ashley waltz lightly across the four-inch beam. When she got to the end of the beam, she did a perfect pirouette. She wobbled a little on her forward roll. I would be doing a backward roll, and that was much harder.

Ashley did a high forward kick. She paused a second up on one foot. Then she lunged into a roundoff dismount, which I was doing, too. She landed without needing to take a step. She raised her hands in the air in a perfect victory salute.

Becky and her friends all clapped.

"Your routine is much harder," Cindi whispered to me.

"Yeah, but she didn't make a mistake," I said.

"You won't, either," said Lauren. "Run the movie one more time in your head."

I tried to close my eyes and picture the white screen, but all I could see was myself falling off when I tried to do the Tinsica, or toupee, as my sister Debi had named it.

The judge finished writing down his score. He whispered something to Patrick.

"Darlene, he's ready for you now," said Patrick.

I walked over to the beam. I started to salute the judge. Patrick stopped me. "Darlene, do you need the springboard?"

I shook my head no.

"Then move it out of the way," Patrick reminded me.

I could feel my face get hot. I went to the end of the beam and shoved the board to the side. Jodi jumped up to help me, but I waved her aside.

Then I took a deep breath.

I saluted the judge again. I tried to smile, but I couldn't.

The judge raised his hand, indicating he was ready to watch me.

I put my hands on the beam and pushed hard.

I needed all my strength to push my legs over my head to do the chest-mount. I could feel my elbows digging into my body, and my legs were shaking, but I kept them tight together. Then I slowly lowered them so that I was straddling the beam. I did a V-seat-balance pose, which is exactly what it sounds like. You try to shape your body like a V. Then I did a knee scale, and I was finally standing on the beam.

At least I had gotten on the beam without falling off. The other Pinecones had told me to do my most difficult trick right at the beginning so that I could get it over with.

I took a deep breath and raised my arms to begin my Tinsica. I pushed off into my cartwheel and then I twisted, lowering my front leg slowly down so that I was in a one-legged backbend. I remembered to point my toes. Then I pushed up and ended in a pose.

I heard a whoop and a holler. It was Cindi, Lauren, and Jodi. They were grinning as if they had done it themselves.

The rest of my routine was easy. I just had to do a little run and then a tuck jump, my backwards roll, and dismount. But when I tucked my feet underneath me in the jump, I suddenly fell off the beam. Splat.

I mean, I didn't have a second to try to catch my balance. I just plain came tumbling down. I landed hard on the mat. I wanted to cry!

I stood up. The other Pinecones stared at me as if they were watching a horror show.

I knew I had just a few more seconds to remount or I'd be disqualified.

I put my hands on the beam and pushed myself back up.

I don't even remember the rest of my routine, but I got through it. I did my roundoff dismount, and I managed not to take an extra step.

The room was silent for a second.

I stepped off the mat, shaking my head.

Cindi, Lauren, and Jodi surrounded me.

"I screwed up," I said, fighting to keep back the tears.

"You did great," said Lauren.

"But I fell off and she didn't," I said. "And I fell off on the easiest move of them all."

"You got back on in plenty of time," said Jodi. "I still think you won."

Patrick and the judge conferred.

Then Patrick raised his hand. "Darlene and Ashley, I want to congratulate you on how hard you worked."

"Just get to the winner," I heard Becky mutter.

The judge stood up. "It was interesting. You both had completely different styles so it was hard to judge. But I declare Darlene Broderick the winner. She had many more difficult elements in her routine, and she is an extremely graceful gymnast. My final scores were 7.4 for Darlene, 6.3 for Ashley."

"ALL RIGHT!" shouted Cindi. She took my hand and waved it in the air.

"I won!" I shrieked. "I actually won!"

"It wasn't fair!" cried Ashley. Her face was all splotchy. She looked like she was having a temper tantrum.

"What wasn't fair?" I asked. "The judge didn't know either of us."

"You had all the Pinecones helping you and I only had Becky," shouted Ashley.

"Ashley," warned Patrick. "That's enough. Darlene won it fair and square."

Ashley grabbed her towel and ran off into the locker room.

Patrick shook my hand. "Congratulations, Darlene," he said. "You really earned the spotlight."

"She's a winner!" said Cindi.

I grinned. I was, wasn't I?

15

I Am a Winner!
That Doesn't Sound Silly

I was so nervous. It wasn't just that my mouth was dry. My eyeballs felt dry. I had been so focused on winning that I had forgotten what it was I had won. Now I had to go out there and do my routine in front of thousands of people.

We stood underneath the stadium looking out at the green grass with the white lines. I had been there so many times and heard the crowd screaming for my dad and the Broncos. But I had never realized what it sounded like when it was going to be you they were yelling for.

"I can't believe we're really here," shouted Jodi in my ear. All the Pinecones were dressed in our white leotards with the evergreen tree on the front.

"I'm nervous," said Ashley. "I've gotta go pee again."

I looked down at her. She was wearing her Evergreen uniform for the first time. Naturally, she looked adorable in it.

I almost felt sorry for her. She had really worked hard on her routine. "Hurry back," I said. "We're supposed to go out there in a few minutes."

"I won't miss it," said Ashley. "Becky told me that she bets you fall off in front of *everybody*." She turned and skipped to the bathroom.

And to think that a few seconds earlier I had been feeling sympathetic to the little twerp.

"I'm so glad it's going to be you out there and not her," whispered Cindi.

"Me, too!" I said. "Me, too."

At least the Broncos were winning. The crowd was in a good mood. The halftime show was already underway. They had saluted the Little Leaguers and the PeeWee football league.

We watched as the ground crew rolled out a beam and set it up on the fifty-yard line.

Dad came out of the locker room. He shook hands with Patrick.

"I understand Darlene had to fight for her moment in the spotlight," Dad said to Patrick.

"She earned it," said Patrick. "You should be proud of her. She's got a winning attitude."

Dad hugged me. "I know, I know," he said.

I listened to the noise of the crowd. "I'm gonna die out there in front of seventy thousand people," I whispered to him.

Dad kept his arms around me. "Just pick out one face to smile at," he said. "Don't worry about the rest of them."

Ashley came back and stood in line.

Suddenly a loud voice boomed off the concrete walls where we were standing.

"LADIES AND GENTLEMEN! OUR SALUTE TO THE YOUNG ATHLETES OF DENVER CONTINUES. WE HAVE A SPECIAL TREAT. THE DAUGHTER OF OUR OWN BIG BEEF WILL SHOW YOU HER SKILLS ON THE BALANCE BEAM. SHE'S A LITTLE TINY THING COMPARED TO HER DAD, SO WE DIRECT YOUR ATTENTION TO THE BIG SCREEN FOR DARLENE BRODERICK AND THE PINECONES, COACHED BY PATRICK HARMON."

"Tiny little thing?" I exclaimed. "They must have thought Ashley won."

"That's only in comparison to me." said Dad. "Good luck, honey."

Patrick headed out. I followed in his footsteps. The other Pinecones fell in behind us. We marched in a straight line out to the fifty-yard line.

All the Pinecones did a roundoff and two back handsprings.

The crowd cheered.

Then the Pinecones all mounted the beam and saluted the crowd.

I saw my mom and my sisters sitting down in the front row. Mom grinned at me. Debi gave me a big wave. Then she pulled out a big sign. WE'RE VOTING FOR YOU. Mom must have written it because Debi's too little to write, but I knew that Debi had drawn the big, lopsided heart.

Then the other Pinecones jumped off the beam and I was alone up there. I waved back at Debi and the crowd cheered. They thought I was waving to them. The cheers sounded terrific. I waved again, and they cheered louder.

Then Patrick patted the beam. The Pinecones stood alongside of the beam, watching me.

It was now or never.

I put my hands on the beam and I did my mount. My legs were shaking, and I almost fell off.

But as soon as I stood on the beam the crowd cheered again. They liked me. They didn't want me to fall.

I did a pose on the end of the beam, with one arm up and one leg lifted. I got another cheer, and I hadn't even done anything yet.

Then I lunged and kicked into my cartwheel, twisting into the Tinsica. I almost fell, but Patrick was there this time to spot me.

The crowd cheered and cheered. I loved it! They liked me.

I didn't fall once!

I finished my routine.

All I had to do was my dismount. I saw Cindi, Lauren, and Jodi looking up at me. They didn't look jealous. They looked excited. Only Ashley was fidgeting.

I took a deep breath and lunged for the end of the beam to do my dismount.

On my landing I lurched to the side and almost fell. The Pinecones grabbed me and hugged me. We jumped up and down. The crowd seemed to love me. We couldn't hear ourselves over the noise of the crowd. I felt like I was burning up inside, I was so happy!

Then Dad and the other Broncos came out to the fifty-yard line. They formed a pyramid.

Patrick gave me a lift up.

I stood on my father's shoulders, way above everyone else. I waved to the crowd and an enormous cheer came back at me.

I waved both arms over my head.

"I *am* A WINNER!" I shouted into the noise of the crowd. And somehow the words didn't sound silly to me.

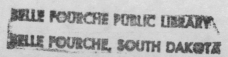

WIN A GYMNASTS WORK-OUT TOWEL!

Presenting...

THE GYMNASTS™

G·I·V·E·A·W·A·Y·!

Working out is fun for the girls at the Evergreen Gymnastics Academy! It can be more fun for you! Enter The Gymnasts Giveaway and YOU can win a big, Gymnasts work-out towel! It's easy! Just fill in the coupon below and return to us by May 31, 1989.

200 Winners!

You'll flip for this towel... and this great series!
Don't miss out on fun and adventure with **The Gymnasts!**

Fill in your name, age, and address below or write the information on a 3" × 5" piece of paper and mail to:
THE GYMNASTS GIVEAWAY, Scholastic Inc., Dept GYM, 730 Broadway, New York, NY 10003.

Where did you buy this book?

☐ Bookstore ☐ Drug Store ☐ Supermarket
☐ Discount Store ☐ Book Club ☐ Book Fair
☐ Other_____
 specify

Name_____ Birthday_____

Street_____ Age_____

City, State, Zip_____

GYM888

America's Favorite Series

THE BABY-SITTERS CLUB®

by Ann M. Martin

The five girls at Stoneybrook Middle School get into all kinds of adventures...with school, boys, and, of course, baby-sitting!

Collect Them All!